How the Mice Stole Fire

A Southern Maidu Story

retold by D. L. Birchfield
illustrated by Doug Bowles

**McGraw-Hill
School Division**

New York   Farmington

It was long, long ago. It was a time when animals and people could talk to one another.

It was so long ago that birds had not yet learned how to fly.

In that long-ago time, people knew fire was important. But they did not know how to use it.

Then, one day, two mice looked across the ocean at Condor Mountain. They saw smoke.

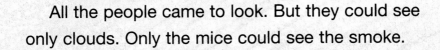

All the people came to look. But they could see only clouds. Only the mice could see the smoke.

"If you can see smoke on Condor Mountain, then go there," said a wise old man to the mice. "Bring back fire for the people."

The mice agreed.

"First, you must build a strong raft," said the wise old man. "You must tie it together with wild grapevines. It must be strong on the stormy sea. Then you must build a fireplace for bringing back the fire."

The mice had never built a raft. But they promised to build a good one.

First, they gathered lots of sticks. Then they gathered wild grapevines and used them to tie the sticks together. Soon they had a good, strong raft.

The mice gathered mud to make bricks. They put them in the sunlight to dry. Then they used the bricks to build a fireplace on the raft. Last, they gathered up some wood.

When everything was ready, the mice set out to sea on their raft.

Condor Mountain was much farther away than they had thought. They traveled all day long. By the time it was night, they saw the shore.

To their surprise, there were many large rafts on the shore. "They must belong to the Condors," said the first mouse. "I knew this would not be easy."

"I don't see anyone," said the second mouse. "The Condors must be guarding their fire."

"Maybe they are asleep," said the first mouse. "Let us try to get fire!"

The other mouse sighed. "How shall we ever get fire? These rafts are so large that the Condors will surely catch us on the ocean."

"That is true," said the first mouse. "Before we get fire, we must plan our escape."

"The Condors cannot catch us if their rafts fall apart," said the second one.

"I know what we can do," said the first mouse. "We must chew the grapevines on their rafts."

So, the two mice began to chew.

When they finished, they noticed a great meeting house. Smoke was rising from a hole in the roof.

"The Condors must all be in there, guarding their fire," said the first mouse. "If we're lucky, they've left their houses empty."

"Let us take care of their weapons," said the second mouse. "They cannot shoot arrows at us if their bows have no strings."

So, the mice went to every Condor house. They chewed through every string on every bow.

When they finished chewing through all the bowstrings, the mice climbed the side of Condor Mountain. Quietly, they tiptoed to the big meeting house. They sneaked inside.

The Condors were gathered around their fire. They were in a big circle, sound asleep. Their wings were touching one another.

A thin wisp of smoke circled up to a hole in the ceiling.

The only sound was the Condors snoring.

The mice were scared. They could feel their little hearts pounding in their chests.

For a long time, the mice watched the big Condors. They looked for an opening. But the wings of the Condors made a tight curtain guarding the fire.

Finally, one mouse whispered, "Maybe we can chew through the tips of their wing feathers."

"That sounds dangerous," whispered the other mouse. "We had better be ready to run."

They picked an old Condor who was snoring very loudly. He seemed to be in a deep sleep.

Carefully, the mice began chewing through the end of his wing feathers.

Before long, the mice had chewed an opening. It was just big enough for one of them to squeeze through.

With his heart pounding, one mouse eased between the feathers. He tiptoed toward the fire. He grabbed a stick from the fire and ran back toward the opening.

When the mouse pulled the burning stick through the old Condor's feathers, the bird gave a loud squawk. All the other Condors woke up!

One of the Condors saw the mice. "They're stealing our fire!" he yelled.

The mice ran down the side of the mountain. They leaped onto their raft. They barely had time to put the fire in the fireplace and push the raft into the ocean before the Condors reached the beach.

Some of the Condors had grabbed their weapons from their houses. But they saw that their bows had broken strings.

When they tried to push their rafts into the water, the rafts all fell apart.

All the Condors could do was stand on the beach and watch the mice sail away.

The mice carefully tended their fire all through the long journey home.

The people were very happy to see them. It didn't take long for them to learn how to use fire.

They learned that they could use fire to cook their food. They learned that they could use fire to keep warm. And they learned that it can make a wonderful campfire, even on a warm summer night.